GRANDMA'S GUN

GRANDMA'S GUN

By Patricia Miles Martin

Illustrated by Robert Corey

Golden Gate Junior Books
San Carlos, California

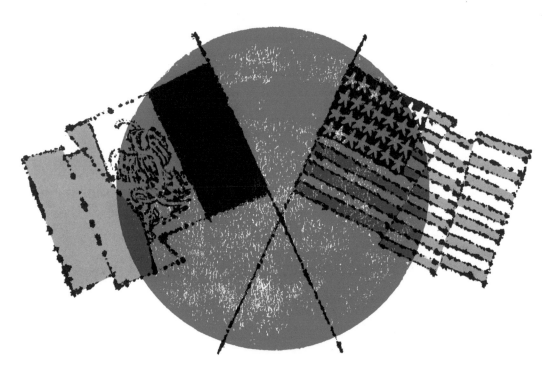

FOR MARK TIPTON

Young Juan lay stretched along a big branch high in an old oak tree. A chipmunk looked at him inquiringly, but Juan did not move. This was not the time to think of chipmunks or rabbits, quail or wild turkeys. This was the time to hide. Through the branches, Juan saw his grandmother stooping over the river's edge as she washed their clothes. A tall stranger stood near.

As he talked to her he pointed toward the woods. He was dressed in buckskin, slick with wear. A hunting knife was tucked in his beaded belt and he carried a rifle.

Juan could not hear what the stranger said, but he knew this man was a scout who carried news of war. And because Grandma knew the secret of listening, she would learn many things.

Always, when she washed the clothes in the river, she waited for scouts who knew about trouble in California, for this was the year 1846 when California belonged to Mexico, when Mexico and the United States were at war.

In this long-ago time there was no mail to carry news. But when a scout brought news, Grandma listened and told the next scout, who told another, and so the news traveled from rancho to rancho, from one Californian to another.

Juan was proud to be a Californian. He thought of all Californians—those brave settlers who came from Old Mexico to find homes in this new land.

Quietly Juan waited in the tree, for he knew that
sometimes a scout would tell his grandmother important
things that he would not tell if a boy were near.

When the stranger went silently on his way, Juan
slid from branch to branch and dropped to the ground.

"Did the scout tell you about the war, Grandma?" he asked.

Grandma wiped her wet hands on her apron.
"Yes. The Americans are coming. Even now they march from the
mountains and they sail by sea. They will try to take the
Pueblo of Los Angeles by surprise. Go to the Pueblo and tell
them. Say that there is no time to lose."

Juan ran through the woods, hardly feeling the branches that
tore his shirt. He hugged the shadows, afraid that the Americans
might be hiding in the woods. But he saw only sheep grazing in a
river meadow and valley quail whirring up beside his path.

He climbed a hill and stood for a
moment looking down on the
Pueblo. He heard music of guitars
and happy, singing voices. Everything seemed as it had always been.

Down the hill he ran, stumbling,
almost falling, sliding, straight
to the plaza in the Pueblo.

"The Americans are coming!" he shouted. "They are coming to the Pueblo."

Young men gathered around him.

"How do you know this, Juan?" a man asked.

"A scout told Grandma at the river. The Americans are coming. They're coming now."

In the center of the plaza stood a cannon. Juan touched the flared muzzle of the old gun.

"Perhaps you can fight them with this," he said.

"The gun is still good," a man said. "At the last fiesta it blasted with great force. We can find balls and shot for it, but we will need powder. And we have no powder."

"We will find powder," another said.
"If we hide the gun, perhaps we
will find a time to use it later."

The men talked excitedly together.

"But where will we hide it?"

"The soldiers will search for our guns."

"They will look in our houses."

"The gun is too big to hide—"

"Perhaps they would not look in
Grandma's orchard," Juan said.
"You could hide it there."

"The boy is right."

Five men lifted the gun to
the back of a great strong horse.
Juan rode with the rider last in line.
They rode around the hill, through
the woods and to his own hacienda.

Around the house, past an old wagon
that stood by a rambling barn, they
went straight to the orchard.

Grandma came running.

"We are going to hide the gun in the orchard," Juan told her.

"There is a spade in the barn," his grandmother said. "You will dig a hole in the middle of the orchard and bury the gun. When you come for it you may take the wagon."

The gun was dark with age. It had been in the plaza as long as Juan could remember.

"The gun is old," Grandma said.
"Perhaps it is too old to be of any use."

"It is not too old," Juan said.
"Sometimes old things are best."

The men dug a hole. They lowered
the gun carefully and covered it over.

Hens came running and scratched
to find the worms that were wriggling
in the turned earth.

"Perhaps the soldiers will not
come here to look for guns,"
Grandma said. "Perhaps
they will look in the Pueblo."

But that night, when Juan and his grandmother
were eating their supper, the mission bells rang a
message of danger. And soon afterward horses came
galloping across the courtyard to the door.

"Unlock," a voice shouted.
"They have come," Juan whispered.
"Unlock!" The voice was louder.
"The door is not barred," Grandma called. "Enter.
All strangers are welcome in this house."
Two American soldiers, one tall, one fat,
came into the kitchen.
"We are looking for guns," the tall one said.
"You are welcome to look." Grandma smiled.
"You will find nothing."

The soldiers looked in the kitchen.
The fat soldier stepped over two lazy hens and
pushed a third from a basket. The hens spread their
wings and cackled loudly in protest.
"There is nothing here but a hen's nest," the fat
one said. He picked up an egg from the basket and
tossed it into the air. Juan wished that the egg
would break in the soldier's hand when he caught it.
But it did not.

They searched through the house and outside in the courtyard. Beside the kitchen door stood a large red-brown water jug.

"Look in the jug," the tall soldier ordered. "That's big enough to hold pistols."

The fat soldier kicked the jug and it broke into many pieces. "Nothing here but water."

They looked in the wagon by the barn. They looked through the barn. The fat soldier picked up a pitchfork and struck it into a pile of hay. "Nothing," he said.

They started toward the orchard. Juan held his breath. They stopped at the first peach tree.

"There's nothing on this ranch," the tall one said.

Juan watched them leave. "The gun is safe," he said.

"And we too will be safe if we stay here at home," Grandma said.

So it was some time before Juan went again to the hill that overlooked the Pueblo. There he found two brothers, Luis and Rodrigo, lounging in the weeds, their hats shading their eyes.

Luis pushed his hat back on his head.
"It is Juan again," he said.

Down below in the Pueblo, a strange flag flew from the plaza. It is the flag of the Americans, Juan thought. He wondered what terrible things this might mean. There in the plaza a few Americans stood leaning on their rifles.

"The flag of the Americans flies over the village." Juan felt sad.

"Yes," Rodrigo said. "The battle was quickly fought. They have left a few soldiers to hold the Pueblo. They need only a few, for they have taken our rifles and they know we can do nothing without our guns."

"When the Americans first came," Luis said, "our lives were much as they were before. But when they sailed away and left the Lieutenant in charge, things changed. He has made laws. No two persons may walk together. We must travel alone."

"But we meet here," Rodrigo said. "We hate the Lieutenant. He plays at being Emperor. We may not play the guitar nor may we sing."

"And who can be happy without music?" Luis asked.

"They have guns. We have nothing," Rodrigo said.

"You have one gun," Juan reminded them. "You have one big gun—the gun in our orchard."

Rodrigo sat up. "You are right. We have one big gun."

"We will find powder," Luis said. "Workers at the mission have often made gunpowder there. It may be they have powder now. I will go to the mission."

He put his hand on Juan's shoulder. "If you hear
noises from your orchard tonight, it will mean
that we have found powder for the gun.
If you hear noises tonight, my young friend,
cover your head and sleep . . ."

But Juan did not sleep. When he heard horses blowing and the sound of muffled voices, he crept outside. Men were waiting in the orchard.

Rodrigo came from the barn carrying a spade. Luis took it from him and struck it deep into the ground. Carefully, the men removed the dirt.

Five men lifted the old gun up and into the wagon. They unwound their riatas and each fastened one

end of his rope to the wagon and the other end to his saddle horn.

The men swung up into their saddles. Juan climbed into the wagon with the gun.

With ropes taut, they plunged forward. For a moment the old wheels did not turn. Then, with a lurch, the wagon started and rolled around the barn, around the house, and across the pasture toward the woods.

Juan rode standing.

They stopped near the top of the hill. Juan jumped to the ground and crawled through the weeds until he looked down on the Pueblo of Los Angeles.

There at the bottom of the hill, clearly outlined in the light of the moon, the enemy soldiers were talking together.

Juan lay in the weeds and watched the men load the gun.

Then everything was ready . . .

Up to the top of the hill they came, and over and down they went, horses and riders, wagon lurching at the ends of their riatas, straight toward the enemy at the foot of the hill.

Luis galloped close beside the cannon. There . . . he reached out with his cigarette and lit the powder in the touchhole. The gun went off with a great blast. The battle had begun.

The riders shouted and turned their horses. Up they came, pulling the wagon with its cannon.

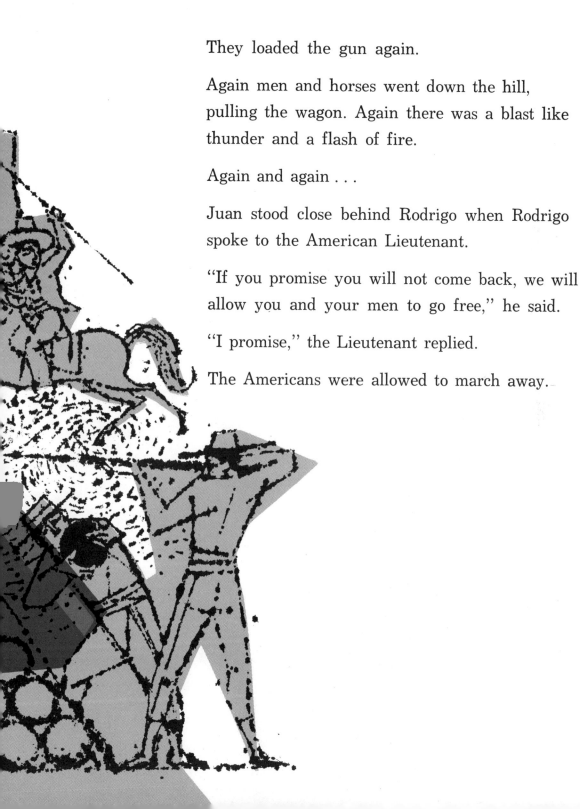

They loaded the gun again.

Again men and horses went down the hill, pulling the wagon. Again there was a blast like thunder and a flash of fire.

Again and again . . .

Juan stood close behind Rodrigo when Rodrigo spoke to the American Lieutenant.

"If you promise you will not come back, we will allow you and your men to go free," he said.

"I promise," the Lieutenant replied.

The Americans were allowed to march away.

In the plaza, the flag of the Americans was lowered and the Mexican flag was raised.

Juan hurried home. "Those Americans have surrendered," he told his grandmother. "The Mexican flag blows out in the wind."

He thought about the big gun with its flared muzzle. In his mind it was Grandma's gun. The men had taken it back to the Pueblo where it now stood in its old place in the plaza.

"There is singing and laughing and music in the Pueblo," he said. "Nothing is really changed."

"Things always change," said his grandmother. "They will come again, those Americans."

It was not long before they came with thunder
of cannon and flash of guns.

They came and they conquered.
Now that they had come to stay, Juan went
again to the hill overlooking the village.

Everything looked the same, except for the American
flag jerking out in the wind.

Have things really changed? he wondered.

Then clearly he heard the bong of mission bells.
And when the bells were stilled, there was music,
soft music of Mexican guitars.